W9-BMQ-632

OLIVIA™
and the Easter Egg Hunt

adapted by Cordelia Evans
based on the screenplay "Olivia and the Treasure Hunt" written by Patricia Resnick
illustrated by Shane L. Johnson

Simon Spotlight
New York   London   Toronto   Sydney   New Delhi

Based on the TV series OLIVIA™ as seen on Nickelodeon™

SIMON SPOTLIGHT
An imprint of Simon & Schuster Children's Publishing Division
1230 Avenue of the Americas, New York, New York 10020
OLIVIA™ Ian Falconer Ink Unlimited, Inc. and © 2013 Ian Falconer and Classic Media, LLC. All rights reserved,
including the right of reproduction in whole or in part in any form.
SIMON SPOTLIGHT and colophon are registered trademarks of Simon & Schuster, Inc.
For information about special discounts for bulk purchases,
please contact Simon & Schuster Special Sales at 1-866-506-1949
or business@simonandschuster.com.
Manufactured in the United States of America 0214 LAK
4 5 6 7 8 9 10
ISBN 978-1-4424-6022-5
ISBN 978-1-4424-6023-2 (eBook)

One Sunday morning Olivia woke up bright and early. "Today is Easter!" she said. "I better go wake up Ian so we can check our Easter baskets."

"Don't worry, I'm awake!" said Ian, who was standing in Olivia's doorway. "I'll race you downstairs!"

Father, Mother, and Grandma were waiting downstairs with two big Easter baskets filled with treats.

"Happy Easter!" they said.

"Happy Easter!" replied Olivia and Ian.

"Ooh, a chocolate bunny!" exclaimed Ian, digging through his basket. "My favorite!"

"Well, you'll have to eat it later, Ian," Mom said. "We need to get going if we're going to make it to the Great Easter Egg Hunt on time!"

"Mom is right," said Olivia, setting her Easter basket down in front of the window. Ian reluctantly did the same. "But first we need to come up with a team name!"

"Hmm, how about—" started Father.

"I propose Team Olivia!" Olivia broke in.

Father chuckled. "Team Olivia it is. Let's go, everyone!"

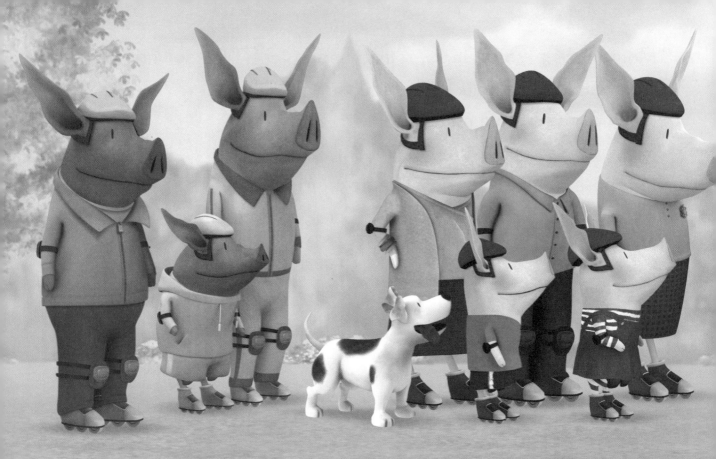

"I can't wait to win this year, Dad!" Francine said loudly as Olivia and her family walked past them at the park. The other teams were all there already, warming up and doing stretches.

Mrs. Hoggenmuller was the grand marshall of the hunt.

"Ladies and gentlemen!" she shouted through a megaphone.

"It's time to begin the Great Easter Egg Hunt! Make sure you have your skates and helmets on because when the bell rings, the race begins!"

"Now, folks, this isn't your average Easter egg hunt,"
Mrs. Hoggenmuller continued. "You'll be collecting eggs, of
course—but you have to complete silly stunts to get them!
The stunts will be at three different locations. The winner of each
stunt will receive an egg with a puzzle piece inside. The first team
to collect three eggs can put the puzzle pieces together to find the
clue that will lead to the Easter basket. The first stunt will take
place at . . . the supermarket!"
And then Mrs. Hoggenmuller rang the bell, and they were off!

Olivia and her family skated to the supermarket as quickly as they could.
When they got there, Francine's family was already there, halfway through the first stunt!

"Welcome to Silly Stunt Number One!" said Mrs. Hoggenmuller. "The Single Strand Spaghetti Slurp! Who will perform from Team Olivia?"

"I'll do it!" volunteered Ian.

"Go, Ian!" cried Olivia as Ian started slurping away.

"Ian wins!" Mrs. Hoggenmuller shouted when Ian finished up the last strand of spaghetti.

"Here is your first egg, Olivia," said Mrs. Hoggenmuller. "And your next stop is . . . the town library!"

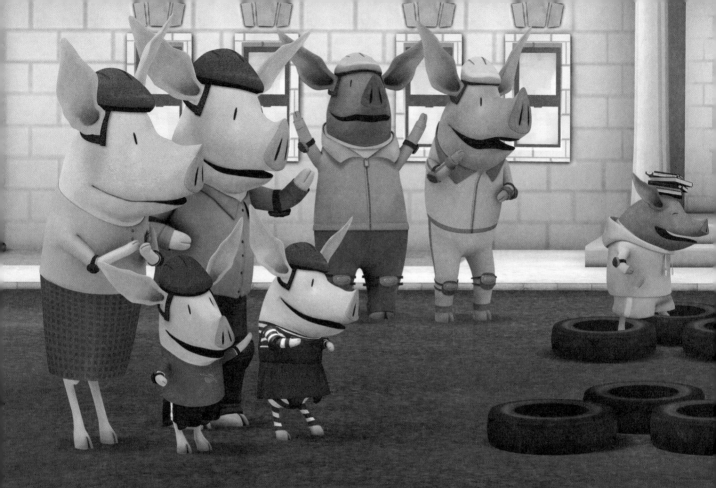

Olivia's family made it to the library just in time to compete with Julian and his parents on Silly Stunt Number Two: the Running of the Books.

"To complete this stunt, you must run through the tire obstacle carrying a stack of books on your head, and then deposit the books in this box," Mrs. Hoggenmuller explained.

"I'll do it!" Grandma volunteered. She carefully placed the books on her head, and began making her way through the tires. "Bawk, bawk-bawk-bawk!" Mrs. Hoggenmuller was doing a chicken impression to test the competitor's concentration! Luckily, Grandma practiced Tai Chi, and was able to keep her balance perfectly.

"Congratulations!" said Mrs. Hoggenmuller. "Here is your second egg. Now it's on to the school gym!"

As Olivia and her family skated over to the school gym, Ian was having a hard time keeping up.

"Come on, Ian—there's only one more stunt to go!" Olivia said encouragingly.

Ian perked up. "You're right! One more stunt, and then I get to eat my chocolate bunny!"

Silly Stunt Number Three was called the Hoop de Loop Challenge. "You need to keep the hoop spinning for one full minute," said Mrs. Hoggenmuller.

"This one is mine, gang!" said Olivia.

"Olivia, you're the best hoop de looper I've ever seen," declared Mother as Olivia expertly kept five hoops spinning and won the challenge.

Mrs. Hoggenmuller handed Olivia the third egg. "Now it's time to open your eggs! Put your puzzle pieces together, and you'll be able to figure out where the Easter basket is," she instructed.

Ian opened the first egg. Inside was a puzzle piece with a picture of a wall on it.

Grandma opened the second egg. This puzzle piece had a picture of a nut on it.

Olivia opened the last egg and pulled out a puzzle piece with a picture of a tree on it.

"A tree, a nut, and a wall," said Olivia. "A wall, a nut, and a tree."

"But what do they stand for?" wondered Grandma.

"Wall . . . nut . . . tree. *Walnut tree!*" exclaimed Olivia. "The Easter basket is in a walnut tree!"

"But which walnut tree?" asked Father. "There are lots of walnut trees around town."

"Look, there's a map on the back of the puzzle pieces," Olivia said. "The walnut tree is in the park!"

Team Olivia raced to the park and stopped suddenly in their tracks.
The park was filled with walnut trees!
"I guess that's why they call it Walnut Tree Park," observed
Grandma.

Suddenly Perry ran over to one of the trees and started barking.

"Perry found something!" shouted Olivia.

"Pick me up, Dad!" Olivia said. Father lifted her up and she grabbed a brightly colored Easter basket that was resting on one of the tree's branches.

"We found it!" yelled Ian.

"Go, Team Olivia!" said Mother.

"The Great Easter Egg Hunt is over, and the winner is . . . Team Olivia!" Mrs. Hoggenmuller announced through her megaphone.

Inside the basket was a big golden egg.

"There's a special surprise inside," said Mrs. Hoggenmuller.

"But you should wait to open it until you get home."

Ian was the first one through the door when Olivia and her family arrived home after the Easter picnic.

"I finally get to eat my chocolate bunny!" he said. He dug through his basket, but instead of pulling out a bunny, he pulled out a mushy blob of melted chocolate and foil.

"Oh no, it's all melted!" cried Ian.

"Don't worry, Ian. You can have mine," said Olivia.
But as she dug through her own basket, she discovered that her bunny had also melted!
"I guess we shouldn't have left them so close to the window on such a sunny day," Olivia said sadly.

Olivia paced the floor, trying to think of a way to cheer Ian up, when she spotted the golden egg in the Easter basket and remembered what Mrs. Hoggenmuller had said about the surprise inside the golden egg.

Olivia carefully pried open the egg and . . . a flood of little chocolate bunnies spilled out!

"Yay!" exclaimed Ian, biting the ears off of one of the bunnies.

"Thanks, Olivia!"

Olivia passed out chocolate bunnies to everyone.

"Great job today, Team Olivia!" she said.

"I can't wait for next year's Easter egg hunt," Olivia said that evening as Mother and Father tucked her into bed. "Maybe we'll get to travel between stunts by jet plane!"

"I don't know where you get these ideas, Olivia," replied her mother.

"I'm going to tell Mrs. Hoggenmuller at school tomorrow," said Olivia sleepily. "Good night, Mom. Good night, Dad."

"Good night, Olivia!" said Mom and Dad.